Ken McCullough
TRAVELLING LIGHT

P O E M S

THUNDER'S
MOUTH
PRESS

NEW YORK

Published in the United States by

THUNDER'S MOUTH PRESS,

93-99 Greene Street, New York, N.Y. 10012

Design by Loretta Li

Photo by Russell Jeffcoat

Grateful acknowledgement to the New York State Council on the Arts and the
National Endowment for the Arts for financial assistance with the publication of this work.
Some of these poems have appeared in one version or another in the following magazines:
Abraxas; *The Ark River Review*; *Corona*; *December*; *The Devil's Millhopper*; *Dogsoldier*;
Free Quarter; *The Hiram Poetry Review*; *Iowa Woman*; *Kudzu*; *Longhouse*; *New Letters*;
North Dakota Quarterly; *The Phoenix Nest*; *The Seattle Review*; *The South Carolina Review*;
Stand Magazine (England); *Studia Mystica*; *Washington Review*—and the following anthologies:
Anthology of Magazine Verse and Yearbook of American Poetry, Monitor Books; *Enter the
Heart of the Fire: A Collection of Mystical Poems*, a book issue of *Studia Mystica*; *I Sing the
Song of Myself*, William Morris and Co.; *New Letters Reader II*, *Southwest—A Contemporary
Anthology*, Red Earth Press; *The Sri Chinmoy Poetry Awards*, Agni Press; *Where We Are:
The Montana Poets Anthology*, Cut Bank/Smoke Root Press—and in *Migrations*,
Stone-Marrow Press; *Creosote*, Seamark Press; and *Elegy for Old Anna*, Seamark Press.
Special thanks to the Helene Wurlitzer Foundation of New Mexico, the South Carolina
Educational Television Network, and the National Endowment for the Arts.
Sponsored by The Writer's Voice of the West Side YMCA in New York City,
the Capricorn Book Award is given annually to the winner of an open
competition among American poets who are over 40 years old.

Library of Congress Cataloging-in-Publication Data

McCullough, Ken.

Travelling light.

I. Title.

PS3563.A2683T7 1987   811'.54   87-6474

ISBN 0-938410-45-8

Manufactured in the United States of America

Distributed by Persea Books Inc.

225 Lafayette, New York, N.Y. 10012

212-431-5270

FOR CHRISTIANA
and in memory of
KATHERINE COSGRIFF MILLER

FOR SWAMI MUKTANANDA
spiritual guide

FOR GEORGE STARBUCK
mentor

FOR LEN RANDOLPH
who insisted I not give up

FOR MY MOTHER AND FATHER
*in thanks for the gifts of
life, love and education*

AND ESPECIALLY FOR KAY
*who believed from the beginning
and has kept on believing*

Contents

I   ELEGY FOR OLD ANNA

    Elegy for Old Anna   3

II   CREOSOTE

    Amish Summer   21

    Joe Miller   22

    Montana: Midwinter   24

    Statement of Intent   25

    Things to Do Around Taos   26

    Under the Rosebud   29

    My Foot Finds   32

    Vespers, Late September   33

    Taking Up the Trail   36

III   LANDFALL

    Fruits from the Outside World   41

    Isle of Palms   43

    In the Summer of the Year One   45

    Venezia   48

    The Moment, and All Such Moments   49

IV   CELLO PIECES

    Buckley Interviews Borges   53

    Lines Written While Listening to Alex Haley   56

    Stopping Along the Mississippi   58

    Earl Miller   60

    In Memoriam, Richard Brautigan, 1935–1984   61

    Apology to Dick Hugo   62

    The Death of 'The Bubble Boy'   63

V   INVOLUNTARY SEASONS

Joey   67

For U Sam Oeur, Cambodian Poet   68

Richard   70

Cal   71

William's Progress   73

Vietnam Veterans Memorial, Washington, D.C.   74

Incarnation   76

VI   CONCERNING THE SOWER

Visitation   79

Looking Out on the Strait of Juan de Fuca   80

Taking the Bus to See You   81

A Vision   82

Rocca Maggiore   85

Santa Clara   86

Enter the Heart of the Fire   87

Autumnal Equinox   88

Instructions   89

Respite   90

Where We Are   92

The Web   93

Responses to Rilke   95

Evening   97

ELEGY FOR OLD ANNA

Elegy for Old Anna

I

A mile from our rented farmhouse
was a ghost town
                    masked from the main road
        by a grove of oaks;
an old church boarded up
                        rusted swings
        a broken bandstand
                five brick houses
and what had been a dancehall

Mid-autumn
                and the air a contrary hive.
        Pheasant hunters
                rumbled by in their pickups,
cut across to the road along the river—
        black Labs in the back
                striking samurai stances.

A white cat
                hunkered on the hood of a '46 Ford
        slim maple shooting out the trunk
                in three directions.

We entered the house nearest the church
                through the teeth of a broken window
        Exposed lath on the walls
                and plaster littering
        the buckled linoleum of the pantry—
three jars of tomatoes gone to toxic slime.
Up the shaky stairs a bed,
                under it a chamberpot
        a plain wooden chair by the window,
        looking out on the graveyard—

                    shutters casting slats
            of light across your body,
                    four months pregnant.
Melancholy settled on the objects in the room
            like silted speech.
                        I caught your eyes and your look
                        let me know that whatever I said
would be the wrong thing, small talk.
                        The sun was going down.
We left, kicking clumps of darkness before us
toward the dancehall.

            A woman named Old Anna
                had lived here.
They'd found her frozen this past winter
                —the thirteen mutts she'd kept with her
                    in the same room
            had nibbled off her fingers.

II
The front is boarded up completely,
                    a heavy silver padlock.
        The right half of the building
                            the dancehall itself
        has collapsed
                and fallen into the basement.
Three gray cats disappear under sodden timbers.
The bricks of the east wall
        have been sculpted by the weather.
I touch one—
        it disintegrates into red dust.

As we skirt the rubble
                we hear voices—

Anna's niece
             and the niece's son.
We are hidden from them by the jungle of ragweed
             grown twelve feet high.
                  The niece and Old Anna
hadn't spoken for twenty years—
        a disagreement no one will discuss.
             I part the weeds to get a look at her—
a twisting red scar near her mouth
        like a worm
             beneath the surface of the skin.
I cannot see the boy.

                  We go in by the back door
             which is ajar.
        We are in a workshop
             with shelves full of grimy gears and gadgets.
I leave you here
        and push on another door
which has something heavy leaning against it.
Just enough purchase for me
                  to get my head around
        to see a long cavern from another era—
             sunken, dank and decomposed.
I squeeze by the door
        pinned by a heavy cabinet
             and make my way through the clutter
        of a fallen stairway.

An old-fashioned general store:
             potbelly filled with trash
        the stovepipe paper-thin
jars of canned goods on the shelves
                  gone gray

petite cartons of Jergen's Face Powder
the color, "Dark Rachel"
three models head-to-head
as in a water ballet
swathed with boas on a white bed
a jar of oil
for washing maching wringers
boxes of buttons
and packs of playing cards
I pick up a baseball bat
browned by the oil of many hands—
Mickey Medwick, Semi-Pro Model
It is so dried out
it feels like balsa wood.
I pull on the door
so you can get through
you show me that the floor we're walking on
isn't dirt—
but a springy layer of dried dog manure
though nothing smells in here . . .
it's like a manger.

III
—only seven months since her death
but it seems that this long tomb
has been unoccupied for ten years.
You'd expect a place like this to spawn
saprophytic life:
dry white spiders
that live on soot—
but nothing stirs.
There are two old divans—
hard to tell which one she slept on.
As the days closed in on her

she became too impaired
        to even shuffle out to the *scheissehaus*
        in the back
she was almost blind, near the end
    and this clogged aisle down the middle
        a comfort to her to navigate—
    her world circumscribed by what she could reach,
her hands
    her only sensory organs.
The objects on the shelves
        and those closest to the wall
    older, less used
        the inner circles of her life
at her fingertips.

Was it the salt the dogs were after?
        or did they think they could ingest
    what it was that had come to them
        through those hands?
Is this where she lay
        when they found her,
    one exposed shoulder
        frail and polished
like that of a young girl?

IV
There is no chronology to the things in the room:
Item: A cookbook, copyright 1898, with elaborate recipes for game—
    including robins, crows and starlings, and a pie of prothonotary warblers.
Item: A stack of *TV Guide*s from 1955—Ed Sullivan, Garry Moore, Jackie
    Gleason, Lawrence Welk, Mary Martin, all in their prime. Odd to see
    things this transitory preserved so well.
Item: A jar of cod-liver oil, with the name HOWIE taped to it. An ancient fish-
    shape raised in the glass.

Item: Sepulchral ledger filled with clippings from the nearby town: who
went to town on the weekend, what they did; who came from
elsewhere to visit, and what was served for dinner—just these and no
others. No written words or other ciphers indicating why they were
kept, or who the people were.

Item: Empty pill bottles, some from the '50s, some with dates just before she
died. None for anything of consequence: folic acid, for digestion, a
low-grade painkiller, a laxative.

Adamant about her self-sufficiency, what had she eaten, anyway? The
canned goods haven't been touched in years, the gas refrigerator, with
its ominous coil on top, minus a door.

Only empty 50-pound bags of catfood.

> Maybe that's what they *all* ate, at the end.
>
> > Or maybe she lived on air and light
> >
> > > like a Himalayan saddhu.
>
> Her life was not *that* simple.

Item: An Edison Fireside Phonograph, patented in 1905, the surface of its
slender bell dappled with rust. Two records, both 78 rpm: Benny
Goodman doing "Benjie's Bubble" on one side and "Gal in Calico"
on the other, and Memphis Jug Band doing "4th Street Mess
Around" and "Papa's Got Your Bath Water On."

Item: A rack of old-lady dresses, which, I think, must have been hers, until I
take one down and see a piece of masking tape with a price on it.
Maybe everything she had was for sale. If the price was right—the river
trader always. . . . for most of us, if the price is right.

Item: A washing machine, with wringers, concealed by a mound of boxes
spewing their moldering contents.

No abandoned family photo album,

> or picture of a President left on the wall,
>
> > no landscape, parched and brown, now, clipped from the
> >
> > > Sunday rotogravure and tacked up and forgotten.
> >
> > > No plastic saint, medallion, keepsake . . .

Alone at night, in broken syllables

to whom did she mumble her deep petitions?
What shape did her God take, along these
simple stations of her life?

V

I widen the lane between the counter and her bed
I wonder how it would have been
on a Saturday at dusk like this
as the shadows lengthened
—the sounds of the accordion and bass
reverberating through the wall
or on St. Paddy's Day, one strapping athlete
drunk in the corner, plays his comb kazoo
already past his prime at the age of 20.
Farm boys, their calloused fingers
snagging the fabric
of Orlon sweaters
during the slow dances.
We waltz our way up and down the aisle
dip and stomp a schottische
to imaginary fiddles.
We stop.
I feel your body working next to mine.
It is almost dark,
the darkness bleeding
through the smudged plastic
covering the two west windows.
Now you would have a smoke—
we kiss instead.   I can see your breath.
The lights of a car come up the road—
maybe hunters returning.
The beams of the headlights careen
across the wainscoted walls
and pass us by.

The nap of her sleeping couch is no longer scratchy—
        worn off with use.
                I spread my jacket for you.
You guide me into you deliberately.
                We make love
                        riding each other in fierce, dark rhythms.

VI

It is twelve years later,
                our son on the verge of adolescence.
        You're in California
                with a husband who shoots skeet
        and does astrology by computer.
Our son lives with me, now.
                I've been back here for two years
        but this time I live in town—
                        my insistence on the natural life
                tempered by the practical
                        or is it lassitude?
Today the kid has soccer practice—
        a chance for me to take my girlfriend
                out to the ghost town
        and see how it feels now.
It's almost the same time of year.
The road there, those eighteen miles
        is much the same—
                no new structures, no timber cleared
                the fields and buildings full of spite

As we turn off the main road
                my heart starts to slide
        the '46 Ford stands as a rusty sentinel
                the crooked maple turned to gold.
A few things have changed: the house

with chamberpot and sickbed has been levelled.
Its mate to the north has been bought by a
                young couple, and restored, as best they could—
they are weavers, and have built a new studio
                beside the house.
And the church is gone
        nothing but the five wide front steps
                and the foundation.
                A gangly pup
        that must be part wolfhound, with trimmed goatee
cavorts with us
                then peels off to lure a Great Dane
        away from his owner.
The Dane cuts a rug in his four white gloves.
                The two play on the steps
                        among the ruins—
        hardly the Parthenon.
Old Anna's place looks exactly as it had—
                the stand of ragweed
                        the boarded front
        the collapsed dancehall.
                        I don't want to go there.

VII
We walk over to the weaver's studio.
                A voice off to the left
                        across the road—
                Anna's niece, some gray in her hair
        and a little trimmer, now
two kids wrestle the family dogs—
        one, the pup who welcomed us.

As we near the weavers'
        a strange long-haired beast

with an underbite
that makes it look Chinese
challenges us with a muffled bark.
One of the weavers, a tall woman
with quick Scandinavian eyes
calls it off.
We go in the studio to look at their work.
The large east window
frames a cornfield
and, in the distance, the house where I used to live
A family there now—
bright garments in several sizes
waving on the clothesline.
I explain to the weaver
that several years ago I had lived in that house
and I remembered a smaller building
I didn't see now.
I used to rummage there
and find old letters and old clothes.
She tells me it was the one-room schoolhouse
torn down about five years ago.
I did not know it was a schoolhouse.
Thinking back, I realize
I must have been unconscious
most of the time.
Her dog peers out from behind her legs.
She inherited it, she says, it is ancient.
It was Anna's, and the mother to all her mutts.
The Ur-dog, cowering politely
in stylized fashion.
Was the rest of her pack like this?

When we were here
we had a rambunctious Lab with a barrel chest

who depended on *us* for nothing
but thrown sticks.
In winter,
he'd drag home the carcasses
of frozen piglets
from the hoglot across the highway.
At night, the odors emanating from him
were cause for exile.
The weaver tells me
Anna's son got married just last month.
And I thought I'd heard he poisoned her
to get her land—
raze the building
and have it clear to the river—
that he'd been smashed up in a head-on
and paralyzed from the neck down
just after she died.
But here it is twelve years, and the place
still stands, as he does.
My own black heart
allowed me that one.
I resent the weaver
for being here—
for having bits of Anna I don't have.

VIII
On our walk back
we turn in at the black wrought-iron gate
wound
with *fin de siècle* curlicues
the name LOUISA above the gate
and the first letter of the last name—G
all the other letters fallen away
maybe sixty graves in here

the oldest from the 1840s
a few veterans of the Civil War
but most more recent
the names: Sweet, Mullinix, Poland . . .
Old headstones for little children
with small lambs resting atop
the features smoothed by rain and snow
—prehistoric lambs
that might have been
excavated at Willendorf,
lone ornamental trees
left to grow twisted and malignant
—they frighten me
like Van Gogh's
cypresses in Arles
ready to burst into flame.

IX
I go to the corner of the graveyard
facing the road—
West.
From here, the river is half a mile,
straight as the raven flies.
The niece had told the weaver
the old woman used to talk about the days
when she was young
and the Indians came in to trade.
You can still pick up points
along the banks
after the snow thaws
but otherwise you'd never know—
pigs and corn.
The river was bigger in those days
and fifteen miles upstream at the next town

it would get a mile wide at flood time.
The channel's deeper now, they say
                    but it never floods here anymore.
                And there were characters like the Iron Man
            a fyce who weighed no more than eighty pounds.
With a rope tied around an ankle
            he'd dive down under the banks
        and poke around until he found a catfish hole,
                    occupied,
            then he'd force his fist down the gullet of the fish,
                right past its spinous teeth
                    and grab on to its guts.
He'd signal with his ankle
                and they'd pull him up
    with a seventy-pounder skewered on his arm.

What was life like for the three of them,
        Anna, her husband and son
            life at full throttle
                with everything intact?
You look at the building now
            and it's an empty hive
        with just one cell
showing signs of life,
        the rest bashed in,
                    deserted.
It must have been that:
            a busy hive—
                the store, the dancehall
        the extra rooms upstairs for revellers.

X
Evening
                the first snow.

15

Up in the timber, the fox
                    barks his doxology.
Out the window, I see
            the neighbor's spaniel
        plunge in circles of uncertainty.
I sit here writing this
                between two walls of books—
        my crutches and crosses—
boxes of trinkets, objects of worship
                magic stones and other documents
        decodable only to me.
                I have been a transient
        following the warm currents here
                a woman's smile there, an eerie sound
                    in the mountains,
        but now, the path of a householder
        new to me, my steps uncertain.
    A life spent crossing borders.
                While yours stepped off
                    into other realms
                or did it?
For both of us, the same
                ragtag museum brought in tow.

The river was the road
                and your town, Anna,
        bore its name.

            I
        must be flying.

As my body's fires begin to glow
                    some to die out,
        I see I can't look back
                    or around

or at.
    I must look in,
       again,
  all the way
      to the end and back.

XI

Anna, my fount or foundling,
    I look to you for sustenance.
I plan to meet your son—
        and listen for the words
           that have your stamp.
As milkweed floss
      settles on the garden
    I will note the nets of memory
      scrimshawed on his face,
his gestures making plain
      what had been obscure
  sink
      in the waters of his eyes,
    and be empty
so empty I remember everything
      as the long afternoon
    tumbles into dusk—
if he would have it so.

I will not return to that heap of bricks.

    But maybe these are lies
        or posturings—
    a veil draped over an unfinished work.
Is this as far as I will go with you?
    Am I no better than a Berber cutthroat
      come to rob your tomb,

The Iron Man
                to wrench you, like a bottom feeder
    out into the light of day?
I don't know if you were free
        or rootbound as you faded.
    Need I look to your son
            to know my own,
        to your marriages and schisms?
I don't know what it is
    I need to know from you,
        or even if I've earned the right
    or ever will.
These signatures you've left me
        say nothing of your eyes.
    When we finally meet
        may I look into those eyes
    and not fall off the face of my life.

II | CREOSOTE

Amish Summer

Tobias, Simon, and I are haying.
A single bell. Black beards move to dinner.

Left by the cats from the evening before
A bat's scapula bastes in its juices;
A hundred and seven degrees at noon.

The bridge planks sob as our buggies cross
The Asian paste of the English River.

My firstborn squints across a field of
Slowly waving corn. His head is like an
Early Harvest apple; yellow, specked, and
Bruised in that one spot, his sockets empty.

Tobias's wife sits with the white cat.
White pigeons are cooing from the silo.
Her face is lamped with the fire of Sodom.

I would walk the half mile down the gravel road
past the pond and the draft horses, past
Irv Chupp's son chasing his sisters' braids
to Joe Miller's place. He'd be in the barn.
He'd hobble out to greet me like a large
rawboned elf. He'd take my gallon jar
and swoop back into the dark of the barn.
He'd settle on a low stool, his gimp leg
splayed out to one side, and start in milking.
He'd squirt the milk directly into my jar.
Every ten beats he'd shoot a stream at one
of the gray barn cats fawning at his flanks.

I might say "Joe, why do those guinea hens
make that funny noise?" He'd say 'K-k-k-kenny,
I heard something . . . now, it m-m-may not be
t-true . . . well, to make a long s-s-story short . . ."
and he'd launch into a wild meander on
guineas and their secret idiosyncrasies.
By then we'd have moved out next to his buggy
under the willow tree. The rasp of the cicadas
blended with the astral whirr of the guineas.
The sun had slid down on the horizon.

I had a beard then, wore denim clothes, and a
beat-up straw, so Joe and the others
regarded me, I guess, as an offbeat
partisan. He might snatch up a copy
of the Amish paper with news from the
colony in Venezuela—that Toby Miller,
son of Daniel, had fallen from his horse,
had broken a leg, but was on the mend.

Joe's job was leading horses into the ring
at the local sale barn. I was there once

when the auctioneer deferred to him:
"Joe, what do you know about this horse?"
Joe lurched to a stop, paused a second,
then said "W-w-well, he's got wind like Fr-freddy
Swartzendruber, and goes down the road like
Ch-chrissy Ropp." The locals got their chuckle
out of that, but he'd given them the goods.

Joe's wife Fanny would appear at the back door
in gray dress, wire-rims, her thick ankles.
With hands on hips she'd yell out "Joe Miller!"
He'd tap me briskly on the shoulder
and say "Well, K-kenny, gotta go now . . .
see ya in a few days," and swing that leg
toward the house with all those cats in tow.

Montana: Midwinter

Winter.
Warm today, though, because of the Chinook.
I have just been looking over some of my old journals
and this has made me edgy.
I leave the cabin to go for a walk.

I follow the little clumps of frozen deerturds,
perfectly shaped,
and come upon a family of blue grouse
sunning on a flat boulder.
The foolhen scolds me until I am almost on her,
then they all roar up into the branches.

I stop to piss in the snow
and look up at the jaggedness of Ross's Peak.
A lodgepole pine creaks in the wind.
I remember a certain swing
on the front porch of an Amish farmhouse in Iowa;
it is summer.
But listening again,
maybe it is more like the sound
the Jeep seat always made on the logging road
when I was a kid in Mississippi.

I am alone.
It is true that I am growing
more each day
like the ones I can no longer
bear speaking to.

Statement of Intent

Like the bitter flight of the tern, like the
hummingbird in his frantic pilgrimage,
my arrival here has been relentless.
I will sit on these stones until they hatch
or become kernels of ripe corn. I will
breathe this white pollen until it cures me.

Things to Do Around Taos

Get up after a nightmare in which some dead men have your house
     surrounded
Wash thoroughly, chant, meditate, do yoga
Eat a lot of yogurt and bananas
Write twelve letters and look over the rough draft of the short
     story you're working on
Put a little cognac in your coffee and pretend you're an aristocrat
Walk into town and go stand around the plaza in your black hat
     pretending you are Billy Jack
Hope that Dennis Hopper sees you and puts you in his next paranoid
     movie
Pay a dollar at the La Fonda Hotel to see D. H. Lawrence's dirty
     paintings, or think about it, anyway
Pay fifty cents to go through the Kit Carson House
Be amazed when you find room after room having nothing to do
     with Kit Carson
Read about what Kit Carson did to the Navajos' peach orchards;
Plan to desecrate his grave
Plan to make a pilgrimage to Blue Lake if you can get permission
Plan to make pilgrimages to Mesa Verde, Canyon de Chelly, Chaco
     Canyon and Oraibi
Plan to do Sufi dancing some Sunday out at the Lama Foundation
Go into the shop next to the Kit Carson House
Have the woman who runs it follow you around to make sure you
     don't rip anything off
Go to the bookstore across the street run by a woman with cruel
     eyes
Buy one book, rip off two
Go to the Harwood Library and look at the death carts upstairs
Walk to the post office in the late afternoon to get your mail
Drop in at Dori's Bakery
Curse Dori's jovial face as you sit there eating pastry after
     pastry

Start home, get splattered with mud by some redneck in a pickup
        just as you're admiring your picture on a poster of a contest
        you've just won
Get home and do some more chanting, some more yoga
Read *The Penitentes of the Southwest*
Sit in the yard with your shirt off feeding crackers to the sparrows
Watch a magpie beat up on a solitary sparrow
Go to the Laundromat and do clothes
Forget to turn the knob from "cold" to "hot"
Be the last one out as the lovely señoritas sweep up
Have fantasies about them as they lean over in their tight jeans
Go home and dress up entirely in black
Go to La Cocina and drink brandy, hoping a rich young widow
        will see you, be impressed, and say let me take you home with
        me and be your Sugar Mom
Make eyes at the cocktail waitress
Check out her profile against the fluorescent lights
Imagine skinny-dipping with her on a moonlit night out at the
        hot springs in The Gorge
Give a skier hard looks when he catches you perusing his bunny
Be awkward when some lady asks you if you've found Zoot Finley yet
Be embarrassed when a member of the group playing nods a friendly
        hello
Wish it was summer
Hear from everybody that D. H. Lawrence was the biggest fascist
        that ever lived
Go across the street and hear Antonio entertain the *turista*
Stand next to a couple from Denver and develop instant rapport
Dance the flamenco with Benjamin, drunk simpático from the pueblo
Tell the couple your life story
Bid goodbye to Benjamin in his blanket as he is being tossed out
Go to Los Compadres and be the only Anglo there,
Finish your beer and leave in a hurry

Go to a dance at Casa Loma,
Feel like a child molester
Go back to La Cocina and ask the cocktail waitress if she'd like
        to go for a drink at Antonio's
She says yes, you go, she finishes half the drink and leaves in
        a hurry
Talk to the guy you're left standing next to about Ireland
Go to the Men's Room and notice you still have a big glop of
        mud in your left ear
Make a date with the barmaid with no intention of keeping it
Sneak out and get splattered by some mestizo high school kids
Get in your mud-spattered battered car, drive home, find the
        phone number of a friend in New Orleans, drive out to a freezing
        phone booth
Punch the phone when it eats your only dime
Drive home again in a swoon and go off the road into a snowbank
Leave the car and walk home to leftover black-eyed peas, a cold
bed, and the dead men surrounding your house

Under the Rosebud

FOR CHARLES AND MARIA SANCHEZ

The elder wakes me, gray moss in his ears,
his hand with four fingers, the life leaks out
of his eyes. The tomboy daughters, now, swarm
around me like doubtful antecedents.
I slip from my bedroll and move toward
our clapboard coffin where the whitetail hangs.
Coffee brewing, the wife with tooth knocked loose.

Last night, the whisky clawing at my gut,
I lurched out under the hunter's moon
to puke in an acre of aluminum;
the largest pile of beercans in the world.
The butcher's voice followed me, telling the
same joke for the third time. His face, his breath
stunk like rotten government surplus beef.

Her purpled braids toward me, I enter
the globe of sadness around her body.
She lives almost suddenly: small gold spoon
falling into a well. Velocity
stains her face; she loves me without mercy.
Every night of this day, those hands like birds
arrive at the tracks of a single horse.

Submerged in autumn, an uncle raises
the poles into place, he smooths the altar.
Three eagles slice the mist above the creek.
I give him some wine and start his pickup.
Three drunks have dumped a trailer in the ditch—
A pair of colts flounder on splintered shanks;
They'll bloat there in the dusty sage tonight.

In the field a convoy of clunkers circle—
a sea of something rolls into my ears.

As my sons chop cottonwood for the fire,
I can taste the sun as thick as honey.
Sage on our palms, we strip and enter the
guest room of this dim museum, sweating
the taut perfume of an unborn nation.

Later, we make the smoke as rain hides down
in Crazy Head. My children cry like gulls
in the detours of the evening. The palm
of powder stabs at the roof of my mouth,
It sings me down this river without oars,
A boat with no one in it. I drink this
distillation of all my body's poisons.

Eyes, black kidneys in a pot, Badger be
my drummer as I fertilize the moon,
Bald eagle dive into a tree of blood,
Coyote, sing your words into my mouth, for
a shaky door is banging in the wind.
Help me now, in this garden ripe with air,
Lift this shadow from the one beneath it.

Shawl of blood and winter sky, the old man
brays the red smoke of his heart into mine;
We fade and become the wind together.
Bleached skull on snake rocks, you lift up your dress
and I look: simple mirrors of your breasts.
A she-wolf losing her teeth beats at the
teepee walls and cannot find the door flap.

Nights I spend more and more time in the air,
circling, inhaling the geography—
a flying snake with the eyes of an owl:
an elk kicks up dust on the trail below,

A goat-bearded man beats his sockets black,
The grandmother's vapors, burial mound.
Over my shoulder, time, and I go on.

I press my ear to this lone juniper,
shipwrecked in the mist. A cold light seeps in
to the murky district of my colon.
We plunge and plunge in each other, locked in
the lips of black flowers, drink the black liquor
of hooves, of hooves, the nipple on my shield:
This serpent has its own tail in its mouth.

Grandfathers rise, their bones bathed in violets,
A sea of horsemen rides across the plains,
The mother turns, and eats her own spawn, we
are making love under the morning star.
Peabody puts the gun in its own mouth.
By the blue glow from the smokehole, we know
we finish last: we are the ones to win.

My Foot Finds

a cedar waxwing

frozen

dry and weightless

under the snow

where he'd fallen, after flying drunk

on fermented chokecherries

into the invisible pantry window

Vespers, Late September

due south, through a gap
    the Tetons
        jut of hip, full breast
   la grande teton
          I can hear
     the song of flowers   driven inward
deep in the cells   a death without complication
  to the west   smoked broken quartz
    intense peach at the horizon
         floating up to pale lavender
    two camprobbers
  voop voop voop in for a landing
     strut   squawk   looking for a handout
      adjourn in brisk jay fashion
to the east   Abiathar and The Thunderer
         stained deep indigo
  Venus appears
      in the crack
    between sundown and moonrise
  a coyote yips
    and his younger brother reports
     deliberate   on the breaths   a meditation
        in a week
         I could break that code
an elk from another planet
        bugles for his mate
    and the wind comes up
      as the moon
        pokes its dome over the mountains
   by now   above me
the Bear rides low in the sky
       looking for a place to hibernate
      the Hunting Dogs yapping at his heels
        Mizar his eye

                at the bend of the Dipper
            and Alcor, its companion
                    barely visible
        (the "human beings" knew them as
                the Horse and Rider)
        the diamond of Delphinus
                        forms Job's Coffin
            Aldebaran
                the Bull's eye
        Cygnus
                hangs there as the Northern Cross
            These designs—
                    mariners and shepherds
                        what else to do
                    with their time at night?
a shooting star   another
        and a third
                so close I expect to hear it
            then a small bright object
                steadily across the sky—
                a satellite
            you can tell the time by
As the stars loom closer
                an electric hum
                        like distant crows
        I am falling up to
            a huge necropolis
                    lit by torches
        my breath   swarms the moonlight
            and I start to chant:
I do not presume to come to this
            Thy table, Mother
                    without my knife in my boot
        I must make my choice

before the wall of ice falls away
If you ask me
   can I identify insanity for you
      I'd have to say
            I've explored the mainland
but my maps might be
            too particular
   like the divine geometry
you've etched on my fingertips
   I travel this new road
            because I want to
      though I do not feel
   or see where it leads
   let it be
      on this side of the river
   let the snow
with its simple thirst
            take time to invent my fragrance

—*Mount Hornaday, northern Wyoming*

Thirty-two below—
I snowshoe up the hill
    beating my hands as they turn to stone.

The sky ahead is   ash

                to zinc

                       to
pearl   to white   —no horizon
through the gauze of drifting snow.
A few stalks of grass in the absence
        bent neatly like bamboo leaves.

Three coyotes lope over the ridge.
    The kit and bitch vanish,
        the male hangs back to decoy;
          I stalk him.

From the top of the ridge
      the winter camp
          a coven of aspen
  smoke from the flaps   bend of the Madison

Pale serum on the Tobacco Roots
    as the sun descends.

I sit on a boulder and
    catch my breath—
  too hard and I'll frost my lungs again

I take one buckskin glove off;
    it is a death mask of my hand.

Down there
        last year in spring
              the river high   I hit a smooth run
        pitched my lure in a hole

        a lone merganser
        complained his way upriver
                and circled back—

        no answer

I looked up at the Bridgers
        tipped in
                    in black and white
    and saw a sassafras
                    somewhere else
basketted in honeysuckle
        and picking hibiscus there
    with my grandson
                before he was born.

My life
        waits for me to catch up.

Alone
        touching the place
    where the answer is.

III LANDFALL

Fruits from the Outside World

1

The first time my arm encircled you
I felt your body's list to starboard:
the spine bunched up in your right shoulder.
I withdrew, I was so afraid for you.
I thought of a friend with the same spine,
a stroke at the age of thirty-two,
ten weeks in a coma, talking to her
later: no more recognition than a chicken.
She recovered, but I felt like a voyeur
palpating your body, wondering how
the organs were pushed against each other.
How close should I let myself get to you?
So delicate, ephemeral, so easily broken.

2

Back from picking dill and parsley for the salad,
the smell of you still on me as I write this.
You sleep, your funny socks, that look like bruised
X rays of your feet, dangle from the headboard.
Your arms around the frilly pillow you've
brought out with you, the right hand open and relaxed,
an invisible cigarette held between the fingers.
I lightly run my hand along your butt,
the back of one thigh: both spring back like moss.

That first night what made you open to me?
And now, whenever I touch you, makes you
back up like a crawdad into a hole.
I can feel you tighten when I enter—
You know I'm gentle, that's not the answer.
You are still the little girl stuck up
in the top of the magnolia tree, high
above the fifth level of the tree house.

Refusing to come down, lobbing inflamed
grenades you find hidden in the branches.

I wait for your darkness to fire, you stir,
your breasts, rare pears: one round, the other an ellipse.
I have the urge to connect the freckles
in the sunny cleavage on your chest.
You lift the flower of your amazed face
and I am witch-awakened once again.

Isle of Palms

The time we ran along the beach
and stopped to talk with a man
musing on half a sand dollar
"Do you ever find them whole?"
      he asks
We assure him, then he talks
of World War II and how the beach was
thirty years ago and how his wife
sits in the rented cottage
brooding at the changes.
We swap small talk, the
football stars of his hometown
you know will strike a chord, then
we both touch his shoulder lightly
and begin our lope along
the beach again, you in the lead
swinging your palomino braids.

Ten strides along we spot
a sand dollar, unbroken.
We pass it back and forth and
your eyes light up even more than usual.

Over the distant pier, over the
whole horizon with the
receding man at the center
the most perfect rainbow
we have ever seen.
Our hands find each other.

We shout at the man and
run to bring him this gift.
The three of us turn

to face the rainbow.
He smiles shyly, a little boy.

It's like this now;
your brightness has gone
    so deep inside me
there are no more miracles.

In the Summer of the Year One

1
As I sit on my steps
            I can hear you inside
        breathing like a dolphin.

The yard of this place
            has fast become a jungle—
the peach trees collapse from want of pruning,
    the peaches squishy and glabrous.
            My figs are blown with flies—
                wasps mine their
        fermenting pulp
then spin drunkenly in the bushy rye.

Yesterday at noon
            a man delivered pears
    to *your* back door
            each one unblemished
wrapped in
        special tissue.

        I go in
    pull back the blue sheet
            slip out of my blue shorts
and nuzzle in behind you.

2
I rummage through your dressing table
    to find a comb for you
uncover a cache of thirteen watchbands—
        an even coven.
Myself,
        I am quick to tell you
        I don't even own a watch—

not one with infrared digital dial
or a brakeman's heirloom, either.
I hate Alligator shirts and Brooks Brothers boxer shorts
don't know one wine from another
and haven't had beluga caviar.
You respond that you're at home
in your Gucci ghetto.
Out the bathroom window
I see the moon
high in the pines
reflected in your pool.
I find the comb and bring it to you.
you run it through your tangled cornsilk
as we walk out in the blowing zinnias
tidy, there, as fancy ladies.
Impatience everywhere.
When I try to caress you
you neigh
and whinny away from me.
I catch you easily.
Concealed by the colonnade, we lean
on the tree they planted at your birth.
Your hands, like ponds
are moving on my back.
As I shift my weight
you sink your dewclaws in
and set the riptides stirring.
You tell me when you were a child
you used to sneak into the pasture every day
and lick the saltlick.
I part your blouse
kiss
your right breast
the nipple rises, hard

as I swirl it with the tip
                    of my tongue.

You pull me down
                    into the dark
        behind the springhouse.

Later, I slip from your bed and go home.

        At my garden
                down by the lake
        I lie on my back
                in the long wet grass
        looking up
and sing to you
                a capella

Venezia

1

At sunset, the gondoliers who have fathers
reappear. They mix the air in stiff arabesques,
make giant candelabras of their oars. Imported
crocodiles swim under the Bridge of Sighs.
I have lost my way in the blind streets with
so many stairways, altars, disjointed swimmers.

2

I have come in search of you, Christina.
If you would have it, for just one season
we could warble on Burano near the tower,
wipe out all traces of nostalgia, begin
the graceful flight above our destinies.

3

It's so simple: I want to live with you;
every day I wake to fight this drowning.

The Moment, and All Such Moments

We shall not cease from exploration
And the end of all our exploring
Will be to arrive where we started
And know the place for the first time.
             "Little Gidding,"
             T. S. Eliot

1

At meeting, the swirling fans were always silent.
Grandma smelled of chanterelles. The beady eyes
in the foxes' heads draped round her neck kept
me from magic sleep. I was in my sailor's suit, Hannah
in banana curls with promises of gum.
Always one at home with chickenpox
splotched with calamine in queasy-smelling quilts.
Outside, our nervous setter pounced on Hannah
after he had wallowed in the sewer.

Plaster fell from the ceiling of the pantry.
Masturbation, butterscotch and chiggers
were the only things I learned that season.
At Sunday dinner, with Mama scrubbed and cantilevered,
the tall carafe became my rosy grail.
Uncle Ted, a thimble of a man,
had slicked his hair with Wildroot.
He once went through this town in style.

2

That spring, traditions grew as thick as flies.
Your eyes would sooner murder than admit
we could be more than kissing cousins.
At dusk, a dozen waiters gathered round
the pool, the bell for tea barely trembled.
Your dear mother grimaced when she saw me—
went back to her absinthe and French cooking.
For her, I trotted out my ancestors

but still, I was a yacht without a mast:
Better to cast my seed in the belly
of a peasant. The others all went home.

You kissed my ear and poured me some Pernod.
I waited for you by the striped gazebo.
Indigo: you dropped your robe by the pool,
your breasts, frightened doves in the moonlight;
you were a mirror that couldn't lie.
The timbre of your whisper rushed like a
trapped snake up my spine: the barrier reef.
The first time I asked you, the sky mumbled—
your answers always were a form of birth.

3

That time we both settled for second best:
I swandived from the twenty-second storey,
you married a balding cotton broker.
But now, in this life, we meet again—
we have, once more, the chance to do it right.
It wasn't I who left you, but the light
inside your eyes that went away from me.

Return to the house on the silent street.
Stand in the arbor, smell cloves in the air.
Do not be afraid of pearls and roses,
the deep music of recrimination.
Mathematical possibilities have little
to do with it. . . . In a crisp white blouse
you listen to the bassoon chortle through some
liquid Villa-Lobos composition.
I inhale the summer gin on your breath.
Why bother with this dress rehearsal, love?

IV CELLO PIECES

Buckley Interviews Borges

FOR RAY DIPALMA

Buckley's tongue rolls in his mouth
in search of a place to thrust itself.
Borges: one eye, the left one, looks up
      the other, straight ahead.
Now that he is blind, he says,
he lives his life with less distraction.
Borges tells of his first translation:
      Wilde's "The Happy Prince"
someone thought it was his father's work
and it was printed as a school text.
Borges then was six;
Buckley shifts his brow back like a foreskin.
I am reminded of a friend telling her daughter
what it's like to have a baby: grab your upper lip
and pull it back over the top of your head.
I wait for Buckley to do this.

Borges rocks back and forth
his left hand flutters from his cane.
His eyes move in their sockets like sad planets.
      The eyes look past us: he says
"I wish I could understand my country—
      I can only love it . . .
capital punishment is kinder than prison . . .
personally I dislike my work . . .
all work is contemptible but doing that work
      is not contemptible . . .
Time flows in an easy way now, for me,
      down an easy slope . . .
laugh off, live up to, live down, dream away . . .
I love all things Scandinavian . . ."

      Buckley closes in on him
he is almost whispering now

making love, they are conspirators
Brutus and Cassius had they survived.
By now the cameras, too, are mesmerized—the two men
        Venusian statues the cameras orbit
Borges says "to talk at all is to make a sweeping statement"
His lips are striated, working like an earthworm.
The tongue flicks in and out—
        he listens now as Buckley
asks questions about Blake, Debray, Márquez,
        Cortázar and Pound . . . there
must be a crumb under his tongue.
He says "when beauty happens, there it is . . .
a thing of beauty is a joy forever. If a line
        is beautiful, the context can be forgotten . . .
Whistler, the transcriber, the onlooker, the misty way . . .
I hate nationalism. I am not a nationalist,
        not a narcissist. A writer
        should not be judged on his opinions . . .
Buenos Aires is a very dull place and
        I am a dull man."
I, listening, have no tolerance for self-effacement but
I love this cello and its grave
        swell of humility.

A friend saw him once at a reception.
He watched, rapt, as every word the right word
        every gesture, itself. My friend
said he never felt more ill-equipped.
Or Burt Britton chomping on his snub Brazilian cigar
telling of Señor Borges's visit to the Strand Bookstore:
Borges was escorted down the stairs and back to
        Burt's lair where they were introduced.
Burt spoke of his own book of writer's self-portraits.
Borges consented. Burt seated him, and said

"Here are the drawings the others did." Borges asks to see them.
One by one. "This is William Saroyan . . ."
Borges nods and makes a sound high in his throat.
          A minute passes.
"W. S. Merwin . . ."—shifts his head forward
        to study it. "Robert Lowell . . ." and on
through the entire stack of drawings.
He was ready, then, to begin. Burt places paper
in front of him and gives him a felt-tipped pen.
Borges sits for some time, thinking, before he begins.
Then his hand moves and the lines appear, precise,
                    somehow.
Twenty minutes pass and he puts the pen down. He says
        he is tired and must rest.
Burt takes his elbow and they go up the stairs.
Borges stands in the middle of the store and listens
        to the room, the stacks, the books:
"You have as many volumes here as we have in our
                    National Library."
Burt will show you the chair Borges sat in. He keeps it
            sealed off in a special place.

Lines Written While Listening to Alex Haley

OR BRENDA RYAN

to our eyes the slave ships
                are empty
the decks scoured clean by
      sand and wind
they cut through the water
                on automatic pilot
now they cross the bar   the slate
      blue of the Atlantic turned brown by
            river silt
but they do not run aground
instead they plow through the sand
      as if it too were water
          air and water
now through the swamps and up the rivers
across forgotten rice fields
              and dormant pastures
      through morning haze
past a live oak wrenched in the
             shape of a cross
they home their way inland
the ground moves   and moans &
           dances begin

In one city at a small black college
          it is Founder's Day
The people sit in ordered tiers
      around the basketball arena
I sit looking out at these faces:
      the cargo of the slave ship
            sustained and multiplied
         the ship become an ark
The speaker
      in tweed coat too warm for the weather

            implores us softly
                    to find our families
            hold them to us
And I hear the ship approaching
        seeking out the genes of those who
                    put us all in chains

Orangeburg, S.C.
March 13, 1977

Stopping Along the Mississippi

FOR JOHN WIDEMAN

I park my truck under some maples
   and open this book of yours, *Hiding Place*
      here in the neutral zone
   where we met back then

I remember you were proud, defiant, ready to erupt
 a sign in your eyes saying DO NOT TOUCH
    —that was in the 60s
  In *Damballah*
   you said you were
  "too scared to enjoy watermelon . . .
     afraid of becoming instant nigger,
 of sitting barefoot and goggle-eyed
 and Day-Glo black
    and drippy-lipped on Massa's fence . . ."
I could sense the edges of your life

      We met again in the '70s
  in unlikely Laramie
    you were still imperious
   but a bit more kid showed through

Now, in the '80s
    we both have sons
   stepping into manhood

Down below me
     the river lumbers into November
 gold
      fades off to mustard
   red to russet

overhead
    a flock of geese
  eases down the flyway

  heading South

Electricity made Earl Miller tick.
Back a spell, in Big Timber, the man who
owned the hardware pressed Earl into service.
Seems a fellow walked by there every morning
on his way to the lumber yard and his dog
tagged along. The dog would stop at the
wooden Indian in front of the store
and lift his leg. Said chief was turning rank.
Earl wired him up. Next day the twosome
trundled by, dog stopped, sniffed, raised the leg
and was knocked halfway across McLeod Street.
From then on he'd cross to the other corner
for the length of *that* block. There was a
Chinaman cooked at a diner used to step
out back and water a certain telephone pole.
They called in Earl on this one, too.
A comic book "Aiyee!" and the problem ceased.
Earl went to work for Montana Power
and the state asked him, as company rep,
to all electrocutions. After a few,
Earl gave others a crack at *this* honor.
Earl drank, which didn't help his diabetes—
died still tough at the age of 74.
Left his wife Kit, sons Roque and Tommy.
When I knew Kit she was a Buddhist by day
but went back to being a Catholic
at night. She took over where Earl left off:
at night, she picked up country music
on the tinfoil round her geranium.

In Memoriam, Richard Brautigan, 1935–1984

FOR TOBY THOMPSON AND JERRY COFFEY

Richard
     disturbed by a horse
          left to decompose
       in the neighbor's pasture
takes a spade
       in the drunk moonlight
     and buries the carcass.
This night
       in the Valley of Paradise
     there is no echo in the canyons
no moon
     reflected on the Yellowstone
       no answers
          augured in the bones.

November 28, 1984

Apology to Dick Hugo

I was afraid that someday somewhere
near the Inner Hebrides the wind
quartering off our stern and a swell

coming up you'd take the tiller and
say to me "So you don't swim much. . . . Jump
in friend Ken . . . I did, and I survived."

These days, I unwrap each of your poems
as if it were a present. No dark
hand waits to seize and drag me under.

Your voice, the thrust of sun through beargrass.
Before, I'd thought you wanted me to
be the tailgunner trapped forever

in a bubble; that I, like you, should
wear that ax-cleft in my forehead as
a mark of penance. Please forgive me.

Mirrors in my kitchen catch the light
and amplify it. I own nothing, Dick,
but the hope that you have given me.

1980

The Death of the 'Bubble Boy'

"David's greatest contribution was his death."
—Dr. William T. Shearer,
Texas Children's Hospital
February 22, 1984

Two lepers huddle in the spring dusk, their ghost fingers
      entwined.

The guitarist sags in his hospital bed, gloves of stone
      crossed mutely on his chest.

Paralyzed from the waist down, the young soldier falls into
      deep sleep, and dreams of the first time they made love.

The condemned man kisses his mistress through the reinforced
      glass of the window slit.

The singer has broken her voice, destroyed her only gift.

The white-haired scientist stands at the tunnel of memory,
      not knowing which way will lead him out.

Beethoven holds the fork in his teeth, presses it against the
      piano. His nostrils flare as the notes resonate through
      the vault of his skull.

And you, David, who lived in a plastic bubble
      from which you passed out
               Halloween candy,
         read books which had to be sterilized,
            watched your classmates by television,
the only break from your cosmic egg
    a lumbering romp on the lawn
             in a NASA spacesuit, which you
      too soon, outgrew,
     and the last two weeks when they let you out to air—

to be kissed for the first time, by your mother,
father, sister, the family dog—
you decide to leave us just before
your passage into manhood.
It showed in your face—you'd lost
none of *your* senses—least of all
your sense of humor:
you winked when they pulled the plug, knowing
something we do not.

Fair sailing, wise one, may our paths cross somewhere
on the distant plains of time.
Seven others like yourself, in seven different cities
will live outside their bubbles, now—
your legacy.
They may feel the blue pulse
leap from a lover's hand.

V INVOLUNTARY SEASONS

Joey

Joey was missing an ear
a dog had bitten off when he was five
but he'd go right up to
my uncle's snarling shepherd
and have him rolling on his back
Joey helped me gather
pigeon feathers
for my Straight Arrow war bonnet
once he got stuck up in a tree
and the fire department had to rescue him
with the whole neighborhood watching
they said he was "hyperactive"
his father had been a cop
killed in the line of duty
we would play monkey-in-the-middle
with my cousin Roger
and the three of us
swam secretly in the green
El Greco waves
behind the groaning ferry piers
The night the Army turned him down
Joe took his old man's .38
off the shelf in the closet
where it lay wrapped
in an oiled cloth
and put the gun to his head

For U Sam Oeur, Cambodian Poet

You came to be my anchor in those days
of chaos, from '66 to '68.
When I was down, which was often,
I would come see you. You would fix tea,
make chicken in soy sauce and wine
with lots of ginger root, and we would
laugh at nothing. You'd offer me peppers
so hot I'd be drunk on just one beer.
I would be better then, brother,
safe within the compass of your smile,
your demeanor so sweetly unlike
anything in *this* world. I remember
when the news came in '68 how you were
shaken, and rose in class to read a poem
none of us could understand. For those
days we shared, you were my closest friend.

I would look through your magazines from home,
stunned by the beauty of your people. You
said if I wandered through a village and
wrote a poem there, the people would build
a small shrine and set the poem in it.
"They worship beauty," you told me.
Before you left I made plans to visit;
we would translate the legends of your homeland.
In your third letter you said there was no
point in writing anymore—all the mail
was censored—things were "disintegrating
fast." I feared for you, knowing you would
not be silent. It was the first time I'd
ever heard despair behind your words.

We often joked about eating dogs—
something you did in your country.

I remember you told me that,
on your way home from a dog barbecue,
all the dogs would approach you
and howl, knowing what you'd been up to.
I can see your impish smile as you
tell me this. Now and then I can feel
that smile floating up behind my own—
I have never forgotten you. But some nights
I wake up howling, because I do not know
if that smile is still a part of you, or if
it was torn from you by American bombs, or
left as dogmeat out in the Khmer Rouge sun.

Richard

Whenever the Air Care chopper
comes in low
over his garden
Richard hits the deck.
Or, when early Iowa summer
gets so green
it reminds him of jungle
he spends his days inside.
His wife, a nurse,
must make a clatter in the kitchen
when she comes in from a late shift
lest he roll out of bed
and open up on her
with an ersatz M-16.
He can't pick up
the beercan flipped in his yard
by a passing teenager
or the wind-blown sports page
come to rest
without the white sear of shrapnel
the tidal wave of fear.
Out-country since '66
he has yet to speak these things
with anyone.

Cal

Cal answered the call of Camelot by
enlisting the day of his graduation.
All his life he'd run with the whitetail,
the antelope and elk. But he himself
became a reptile, obsessed with the strike.
He emptied his piece in the back of a GI
when he found him raping the corpse of a
girl who looked to be no more than 13.
He and a buddy wasted a sergeant
perched atop a tank they were trailing
because the man was a first-class menace.
When a mortar round fell on a shavetail
just assigned to Cal's platoon, Cal laughed.
But one afternoon he found himself
cradling his own smelly guts. Two medics
bought the farm dragging him back to a slick.
He came home in time for a feud between
cowboys and freaks. One night he saw a longhair
surrounded by snoose-chewing buckaroos
preparing to saw some hair with a knife.
Cal stepped down from his pickup and levelled
a 12-gauge at their heads, his eyes black,
his nose hairs glistening. Didn't say a word.
Cal took to dropping acid, and tuned the spokes
of his bike so that when he played them
they sounded like Saigon in a rainstorm.
He couldn't keep his hands off a woman
even if she might be sitting next to you.
When he'd come in at night, his wife would
go down on him, just to find out where he'd been.
He's a guide now, but he pukes whenever
he guts a buck, and after a pint of gin
and some raw deer liver, he'll dance with
antlers on his head and paw the ground.

Once a month he checks in with the VA shrink
to prove he's still 90 percent disabled.
Last I heard, he's got a new wife, and uses
a sluice to flood his garden, paddy-style.
His first wife has a court order to keep him
away from their son, who plays the oboe.
Cal's Mom still slings hash down at the depot.

William's Progress

According to the Marine recruiter
William had a future in computers;
the MOS he got was rifle grunt.
In the Trenton ghetto, the only hunt
he'd been in was for the hottest date,
but now he hunted Charley. The live bait
was Bill. Two purple hearts and 20 missions
late, he took a slow boat stateside—visions
of maggots danced off the stern as he stared,
stoned, into the drink. He was not prepared
for the spangled twelve-year-old who spit
on him in 'Frisco. William quickly split
to Greenville where his grandma helped him heal.
But he needed to move at night, the feel
of a piece on his hip. He took the job
of cop, in Birmingham. Broke up a mob
and clapped the cuffs on a honky—the year
was '67. He had shown no fear
but they took his badge, and he couldn't get
another steady job. That fall he'd met
the girl of his dreams—somehow they made ends meet.
They had a son, a daughter. Life seemed complete,
but William's soul went AWOL. The staves flew
off the barrel; he had to leave. A new
start, again—he got a degree in Psych.
Nights, as a DJ, he'd sit at the mike,
voice smooth as that of a maître d'.
And then he set out after his Ph.D.
until the lesions began to appear
on his arms and legs to ring in the year.
Not eat, not answer the phone, not go
outside, not even let his grandma know.

Vietnam Veterans Memorial, Washington, D.C.

FOR JIM MCGREEVEY

1

Taking the path at night
you come upon it suddenly
lit, as if by candles.
The wall begins in the grass next to you.
You see the first few names, etched in white.
Smooth blackness directs you down
until the weight stops you—
deep in the Valley of Death.
And all the names, the names
cry out!

2

They look across morning haze
        at the black wall with its names—
                an intake of breath
                as they are stopped:
    three GIs in combat fatigues
            their eyes burning
                        and burned by life
            too long at the edge.
The hand
    of the GI in the center
        imperceptibly
                holds back his buddy
        the hand
                of the third man
            goes to the shoulder
                of the central figure
to console him.

3

A man drops quickly to one knee
       in front of the wall
   and the chiselled runes
      that drive a stake through his soul
    deposits his medals
        and walks away.

A grizzled expert in Slavic languages
      in town for the MLA
    rumbles by self-consciously
       spilling popcorn as he goes.

4

The reflection
    of Lincoln's memorial
  appears in the face of
      one wing of the wall
    Washington's monument
       looms in the other.

December 29–30, 1984

Incarnation

A
sacked cathedral
arousing the flight
of the sanest
among us,
who have sunken,
as conscious bait
in a cold, deep lake:
the recognition
of the black
vacuum,
freedom.

A shrew's heart
explodes,
or a nightingale
flies straight up
until it dies,
and falls
into our own
involuntary seasons,
the forlorn sea,
turning
and yielding up
her dead.

VI CONCERNING THE SOWER

Visitation

FOR ROBERT E. MCCULLOUGH, 1908–1972

On the beach, November, cold and alone, I lay there
looking up. I sensed you there and pushed to bring you
into focus. I started to cry and I could not cry.   My
face was scrunched up like a baby's. It was trapped
inside me—a belt around my chest, a hand at my throat.
I called to you for help and you were there, above me
in the air, as you looked at maybe 42, your eyes dark
and glistening. I told you that I had been the way I was
with you: recalcitrant, bristling, itching for a brawl
because I was afraid of you, afraid of becoming you—
a shy countryboy who crumbled cornbread in his buttermilk
who knew nothing but work from Day One, whose only vices
were being too honest, too generous for your own good.
I could breathe now, sighing, and my eyes were open.
I said I understood now, where it came from, the fear
and that I accepted you, now, and wanted you to be with me.
That we never talked, is done with—no guilt on either side.
I have not been able to accept what *I* am yet, and where
I came from.   I want your help.   I need you.
I held out my arms to you and you moved down
toward me steadily, and I could see your eyes as
you approached, fixed on mine—the reflections of me
lying there, confused, snotty-nosed, helpless, and you
merged with me in a nimbus of light, and I wrapped my
arms around you as you came to me and I sobbed, deep and
long, and thanked you for letting me let you in, at last.

Edisto Island, S.C. 1978

Today I left the crowd of picnickers
and walked along the beach toward the cliffs.
The Pacific hissed out beneath the pebbles.
There were chartreuse sea cucumbers and red fronds
waving in the brackish pools—underwater
gardens anchored in the rocks.
I became an intense boy, my eyes
magnifying glasses, and I couldn't
help but think of you, my son.
I move on, a step ahead of my tears.
On the hills above the cliffs is a
pueblo of burrows—domestic rabbits
set free, gone feral, now.
I climb the cliffs, a twisty madrona
affording me a scant windbreak.
I pick through the scattered skulls and legbones
the eagles have left outside the burrows.
A Heathcliff, basking in my grief, alone,
I pocket specimens to bring you when I visit.
Life is a silence, as well as an art—
Teach me what to leave out
and I'll accept the rest of it.

Taking the Bus to See You

Sealed off in this specimen jar on wheels
I smell nothing, taste only the flannel
residue of my breakfast hotcakes.
Mid-morning: we sweep through orange groves, a plump
Chicana with bleached hair brays at her kids—
this is no experience of time and space;
my life, by now, should show me more respect.

Five months ago we spent a week together.
I read a book to you about Giotto—
as I pronounced the Italian names, you
conducted them precisely with your eyebrows.
Your eyes were clear, intense creatures, your breath
quiet on the hairs of my arm. Almost
nine, then, and fast becoming my chameleon.

I see the cross-section of a juniper trunk—
the wood is reddish, the heart wood darker and hoof-shaped.
In the outermost ring I see a man
disappearing into a grove of Douglas fir
He reappears. He is distinguished—
white hair and a curved white beard
His eyes are dark—Persian, probably
and he wears a dark brown robe with the hood thrown back
His expression is haughty—he is annoyed
that I have sought him out in this place
where he is so carefully sequestered
but that look lifts and another replaces it
as if to say "Well, if you were clever enough to find me,
I have no choice but to grant you an audience."

In the second ring, I am on another planet
it is sunset, or some-kind-of-set
the horizon is purple-black and there are
trees silhouetted against it that look like acacias
In the sky are at least fifteen moons
I think to myself "you must be
inventing this as you go," but as I
study the moons I see that each is clearly defined.

In the third circle is my lover, just stepping
from the tub of an old tiled bathroom with
high ceiling and rounded fixtures: Charleston.
I can smell spring blossoms outside the window.
Her eyes are the startling blue of cornflowers—they are
intensely wide and loving, but those of a predator, also.
The towel wrapped around her long blonde hair
is the same color as her eyes. She
fixes that look on me.

I am at the center, now, and it is the heartwood again
but it is not hoof-shaped, I realize, but heart-shaped
Suddenly I am moved backwards at a speed
which dizzies me.
Now it is the heart of Jesus, glowing through his transparent
flesh. I was raised to distrust all religious art
especially the garish statues—where has this come from?
He hovers about three feet above the ground
of a rocky hillside. There is a scraggly tree behind him.
A high wind roars in my ears—
it makes his garments ripple. His outer garment
is cream colored and of a coarse muslin
beneath it is a tunic with vertical stripes
the colors of the rainbow. His right hand is raised,
the left, lowered with the palm open toward me.
The light coming from his eyes is so brilliant
that I can barely distinguish the features of his face
It is like looking at the sun behind a cloud—
the discs of his eyes. I am afraid to
look for too long, to be blinded by this eclipse
My body begins to shake and I am sobbing
The guide says "What you see now
is what you are at your innermost level.
Remember all the details of what you have seen
so that you can call them up when you are in need of strength.
The other rings stand for what you are
from the outside in. Remember these things."

Three months later. Florence, Italy.
The San Marco Monastery. It was here
Savonarola spent his last years as abbot
before they burned him at the stake.
Later, Charles (fellow saddhu) and I
will sit in his meditation room

after looking at his books with his
neatly-penned marginalia, his hair
shirt, his breviary. Hanging above the desk,
his portrait by Fra Bartolommeo, hooded and beaky.
We collapse in opposite corners, meditate
for an hour, looking, I imagine, to other tourists,
like the zapped soldiers guarding The Tomb.

But that was later. Now I mount the stairs
on the way up to the monks' quarters.
At the head of the stairs is Fra Angelico's *Annunciation*
I have seen it so many times, in my head—
the elegantly-crafted wings, the garden,
the smooth whippet faces of Mary and the Archangel—
that my reaction is cool, intellectual. It is
an aetherially fine artifact well-suited for study.

The building is spare but stylish—
if you had to be a monk and in the city,
this would be the place. Each cell, I am
surprised to find, has a fresco by Fra Angelico;
powerful objects for meditation.
When I get to cell number six,
the cornermost cell, I peer in and
there it is—*The Transfiguration of Christ*!
Hovering, with the same wind rippling his garments
flanked by saints recoiling at his power—
Moses, Paul, Francis, etc. the right hand raised.
So much bright yellow light and movement
coming at me from the fresco that I am
driven to my knees. When I can finally stand
I move to the wooden bench where I remain transfixed.
When Charles happens upon me, he asks what
I have been doing. I can only shake my head
and point. He takes a place next to me on the bench.

Rocca Maggiore

Across the Umbrian plain, the basso trill
of combat, horses rear and whinny, metal
rings off metal: Perugia, 1203.
Today, I stand on this jonquil-covered hill
swilling the breeze. The scent of fennel settles
on the town below: Francesco's Assisi.
At any moment I expect a giant
to lope over the horizon—all of it
cut from a fairytale. I turn. Behind me,
at the foot of the steep slope, itinerant
sheep graze the green open valley. It is lit
like a country farther to the North. A hermi-
tage, snug, across the winding Tescio.
I know that Francis saw it once this same way,
stumbled down the hill to camp beneath the stars.
The castle ruins closed today. I follow
the back wall along a narrow path to a
dip in the wall. The muskiness of sheep tars
the air. The clank of their bells behind the wall.
I pull myself up the stones, vault down inside
the pen with them—a thief looking for a place
to roost, prodigal on the run. Two ewes call
their lambs, the others just ignore me. I slide
out of sight. One lamb nibbles at my bootlace.
The caretaker must live here. Through a narrow
gap in the fold I see, framed by a window,
a woman stirring something on the stove, three
thin girls chattering like a flock of sparrows.
I sneak back over the wall. The sun is low
in the West. The frank bouquet of fennel frees
me on the way back to my hotel. I write
a note to my friends, stuff some apples in my
sleeping bag, and hurry, in the fading light,
down the hill to the river to find my camp.

In the crypt of the basilica
of Santa Clara
her body lies in state
in a glass casket
bones of her face
protrude through black leather skin
teeth
through taut-pulled lips
the purity of her soul
keeping the body
from decay
these 700 years
I approach the other hooded figure
behind the window
her hands, her face
concealed in the
folds of her shroud
my turn
step forward
a voice from the hood
crisp
on the microphone
makes the hair on my neck stand
I have heard this voice before
don't understand the words
but the voice
I know it
She finishes
and is waiting
I return from my confusion
to this place
make a donation
move away
for the next in line

Enter the Heart of the Fire

When St. Alonzo staggered through the shallows
he did not see, at first, the questions
in concentric circles, nor the players in completion.
He fell more slowly as he continued not to speak;
a slave by any other gate would take precautions.
Just before his Self's extinction he found the grotto.
Overhead, through hewn passageways
he finally knew their language, then
getting into the boat, the leather of their bodies.
Each of his senses stationed around him
as statues he could barely gloss.
He was not entitled to bloat upon his own devotion;
no time to congratulate, no time to weep.
Free to be loved, he rose above the gardens.

Autumnal Equinox

FOR CHARLES RYAN AND JOE DON LOONEY

years ago
at Svargashram
on the Ganges
at floodstage
the water
opened
and my guide
sitting placid in twilight
warned me
one step farther
and I'd be
swept away forever
a monkeyman
hid from me and
laughed a monkeylaugh
the silt
settled
the sand glowed
my guide's
eyes rolled back
showing only whites
wraiths
drifted among the dogs
the water
opened
I turned and saw
a black angel
on Lakshman's Bridge
sway with its
herd of goats
heading home

Instructions

FOR SHIVANI ARJUNA

Invite them in, these travellers
some with scars across their faces
others no more visible than blue smoke
whether their light flickers
or is so strong that you must turn away—
wash this one's feet, give that one
what you have, even if it's everything;
the days of love, the seconds, are not
numbered—what goes from you comes back
sevenfold. If you have to, run across
the surface of the water, but
for God's sake be quick about it.
When you're up to it, engage Death
in small talk, about the weather,
anything, then see if you can
trick him into turning inside out.

noon on the pipeline—
  break for lunch
    from stringing pipe
      across a muddy creek

on the west bank
  Martin, our porky foreman
snoozes off last night's hooch again
    under an apple tree
      old and fully shaped
his face covered
   by his polkadotted cap
  all but the stubbled
      double chin
I lie back
  against the tire of the compressor
    narrow my eyes
      against the sun
 and sip peppermint tea
wasp
  perches on the lip
 of my thermos

I look at Martin again—

    though it be mid-September now
   the apple tree is festooned
     with white blossoms
  and the empty field
    a riot
      of white and purple clover
Martin himself
  in a body 20 years younger
   glows

with a clean light
I can smell from here

Where We Are

the cornfields   surround us
    bald road   to lowered sky
wind   eating darkness
      a chatter
  of an ocean   growing
    Yet it is   alone   empty
   uprooted again
              pungent   brittle
      to recognize   the black earth
the pull   the anchor
    fixed

      and struggling up

for George Oppen

The Web

Dale Burr, indebted farmer, Iowa, shoots his wife, neighbor, banker, then himself—the doctor says there's nothing on the EKG, but he can hear it in your chest—a sucking murmur in the valves. Now, even when they clean your teeth, you must dose with penicillin three days ahead of time.

Terrorists, Palestinian, Rome airport—fourteen dead—a blood vessel in your brain begins to distend.

Oilman, Houston, suggests that the fetus be untimely ripped from the womb of his significant other—small white blisters appear on the privates of the daughter by his first marriage.

Mengele's skull exhumed in Bolivia—a *Fräulein* in Wiesbaden gives birth to a son with no arms, and eyes that do not see.

Deformed fish bob to the surface of backwoods lakes in northern Maine— the magnate's brother, Pittsburgh, popped for trafficking in heroin.

Antelope, Oregon—if you can't love the one you want, then love whoever stirs your hormones—telltale suggestions register from another dormant volcano.

Software salesman, San Diego, fifth degree black belt, smashes his girlfriend against the freezer and her lights go out for good. Both your hands experience numbness—diagnosed as carpal tunnel syndrome.

Some high school jarheads, Daytona, send foul-mouthed hate mail to their math teacher, Vietnamese. That night, the little brother of one of them has all his teeth caved in—berserk veteran, random incident, convenient store. Mars conjunct with Neptune and Beelzebub.

Bethesda, country club surgeon who's ruined the lives of his wife and twin sons—a chronic alcoholic—is hit head-on by a drunk taxi driver—a short slash you haven't noticed before incised across the life line of your left hand, the one you use the most.

You visit your uncle in the VA hospital, cancer of the throat. He smokes Camels through the hole in his neck. Your nephew, born with spina bifida.

Soweto, several black children die in a fire set by white supremacists. On the way home the whites hear of the airline crash, their families charred beyond recognition—a flight back from the Holy Land. A small brown spot shows up near the center of your right iris.

Marketing exec, former bomber pilot over Cambodia and Laos, works late
    with his private secretary, in a motel, Atlanta suburbs, while his wife is
    butchered by a burglar.
Prim owner of department store, Toledo, buggers a ten-year-old and his ail-
    ing mother falls in the tub and drowns. You notice a sharp pain just below
    the ball of your left foot, that won't go away.
In Ethiopia, children disappear into their skulls,
    and Reagan develops cancer of the colon.
                    the little children suffer—
        suffer the little children unto Me
            inasmuch as you do it unto the least of mine
                    you do it unto Me
            you do it unto yourSelf
        Calcutta, Manila, Managua
            Belfast, Beirut, Kabul
Manson, Sirhan, Ray, Oswald, Ruby are reborn as snails and served to the
    rich in arrogant French restaurants. You eat what you are.
When *you* die, your flesh will be canned as dogfood for policedogs, your
    bones for flutes and awls to villages in Hudson Bay, your vertebrae for
    necklaces in Borneo, your voice, your words, melted into hightech
    glossolalia, beamed to outerspace, to wander, lost, forever.

Responses to Rilke

I
the work:
    you must take up your cross
  to walk the earth
      not sink beneath its surface

II
I hear you sing
      that song
   and I am trapped inside your voice
  like a bird flown in
      at the window
    of a sagging station house

III
summer afternoon
      from a train
   I spot Eurydice, indistinct
      in a fallow cornfield

IV
the eighty window spaces
      of a farmhouse
  broken
    for both our generations

V
an orange
      blue with mold

VI
the early self-portraits
    were of the eyes
      rooting behind them

then, later, as he turned
it might be the flat
triangle
at the base of a woman's spine
or a cropped hump
of marsh grass
in the beach light of morning

VII
the stars crank around
on a warped windmill
the husks of evening
catch slowly in my throat

VIII
I step into the water
and swim easily toward my death

with your arms around my shoulders

Evening

And then,
my dear,
came acceptance.
Then came
hours, days, and
an end of resurrection.
You slept
in the country,
crystal warbler
withholding life.
Singular,
fallible,
you drank
the mating sycamores
the cloud
drifts—
a drink
too heady
to be denied.
Rejoiced,
despite it,
despite the pastels
shredded
by the life-breath
of the farmhouse.
To come,
as we come,
to the full table.
Such a long wait.
Such a
winning over
of terrors
from the mutable.
And then

such a deep
opening
of the moonlight.

About the Author

Ken McCullough was born in Staten Island, New York in 1943. His formative years were spent in Newfoundland. His early influences were Elvis, Mickey Mantle, and Dylan Thomas. He taught at Montana State University, the mountains of Montana becoming his spiritual home. He worked as a writer-producer for South Carolina Educational Television, and as a union laborer. He was a fair southpaw, finally giving that up at semi-pro level at the age of 35. His previous publications are *The Easy Wreckage, Migrations*, and *Creosote*. He received the Academy of American Poets Award 1969, and a National Endowment for the Arts Fellowship 1974. He currently lives in Iowa City, Iowa with his son.